This book belongs to:

Orange Blue Publishing

Copyright 2019 by Beatriz Rare

Cover and illustrations by Beatriz Rare

May 2019, Irvine, California.

It's Not Easy
Being a T-Rex

Written and illustrated by

Beatriz Rare

Hi, my name is Brian.

I'm a T-Rex!

I'm a small one. I have a big snout, a long tail, and tiny arms.

Every T-Rex has tiny arms.

This can be problematic for some activities,

but I always find a solution.

For example, I was very sad when I tried to play baseball.

I couldn't swing the bat because my arms are tiny!

What other sport could I play?

I found the solution!

My legs are very strong, so I'm great at soccer!

I wonder what other sports I'm good at?

My birthday was last month. I wanted to cut a piece of cake.

I stretched my arms as far as I could, but they are tiny!

How could I eat my cake?

I found the solution!

I took a huge bite with my big mouth!
The cake was delicious.

There must be other foods I could eat with
my tiny arms and big mouth, right?

During a party, it was my turn to hit the piñata.

But I wasn't strong enough to break it with the stick.

What else could I use?

I found the solution!

I jumped and hit it with my tail.

It was strong to break the piñata! I wonder what else I could do with my tail?

The other day I tried to ride a bike, but my arms are too tiny!

I couldn't steer the wheel. What else could I ride?

I found the solution!

Not only are my legs strong, they are perfect for skateboarding!

I wonder how else I can move quickly?

Once I tried to make my own pizza, like I saw in a movie.

But I couldn't spin the dough because my arms are tiny!

Actually, I discovered I could spin the pizza using my snout!

It was hard, but I did it anyway.

I wonder what else I can spin on my snout?

Sometimes I wish my arms were longer.

Certain things would be easier.

But I do have a...

big snout,

strong feet,

and a long tail!

I'm a T-Rex,

and I'm awesome!

Other books in the series:

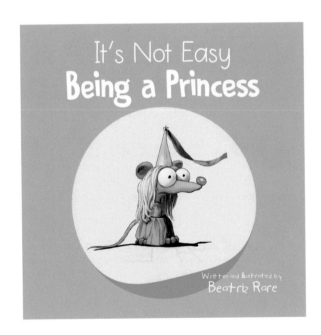

It's Not Easy
Being a Princess

Written and Illustrated by
Beatriz Rare

Other books by the author:

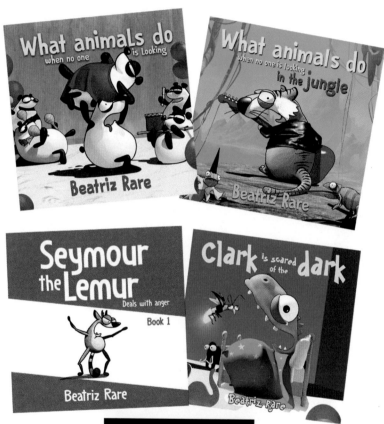

Made in the USA
Middletown, DE
28 May 2019